Miguel's Amazing Book Adeventure

Written by
LaMarr Darnell Shields

Illustrated by

Nathaniel Johnson

Book design by Natalie Estelle

For my son,
Mosiah Sekou Samuel Shields,
and all the special boys who love to read, too!

On a cold and rainy day, Miguel wasn't allowed to go out to play. So he sat in his messy room, with a look of gloom.

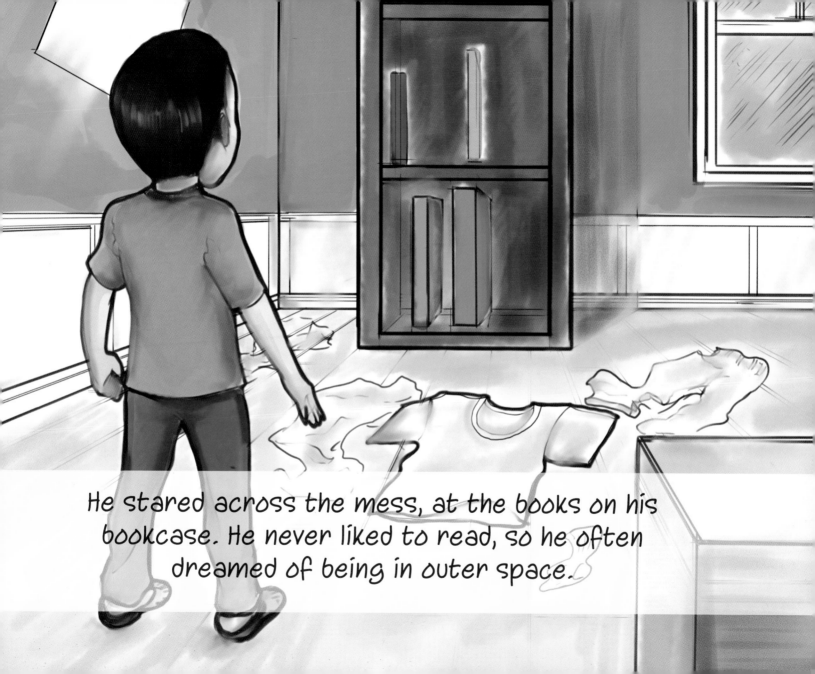

He stared across the mess, at the books on his bookcase. He never liked to read, so he often dreamed of being in outer space.

Boys Read, Too!

I am a boy, and I read, too!

I have BIG dreams, and so should you.

I promise to read everyday and every night.

I know it's the key to growing up right.

Reading books is the best thing I can do.

I will prove to the world, that boys read, too!

-LDS

He thought to himself, "wow, I've never seen this book before". So, he picked up the book, but didn't know what to do, and then suddenly he saw pictures of characters he thought he knew.

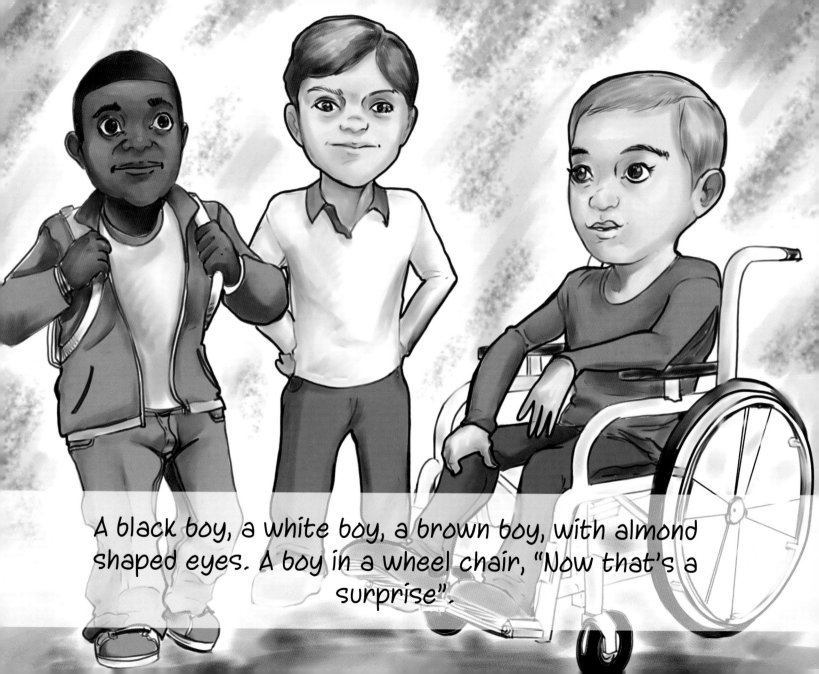

A black boy, a white boy, a brown boy, with almond shaped eyes. A boy in a wheel chair, "Now that's a surprise".

A smart boy, a skinny boy,
a boy with a funny name.

As he began to read more, he thought to himself, "Now this is strange." As he turned the pages to find out more, nothing could have prepared him for what was in store.

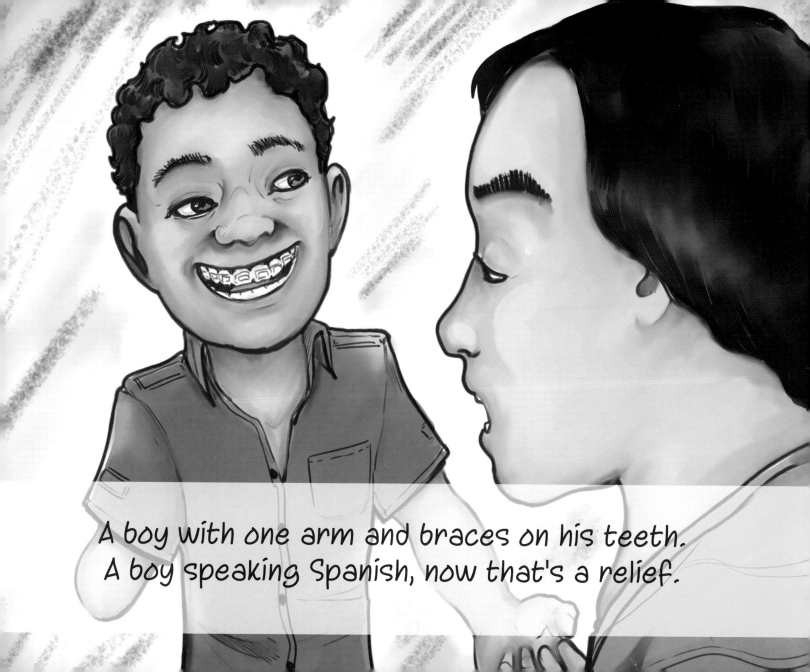

A boy with one arm and braces on his teeth.
A boy speaking Spanish, now that's a relief.

Bravo! Estupdendo! he began to shout. Finalamente! a book about me now that's something to baile (dance) about!

A boy with braids and one with locks in his hair.
A boy from Africa, "I've always wanted to go there."

A boy with two dads, now I wondered how could that be? Then I remembered the conversation between mommy and me.

A smart boy with autism.
A clumsy boy with no rhythm

A boys who's tall, and another who's fat.
A boy with a peanut allergy, and one allergic to cats.

A shy boy, a cry boy,
a "you can't play with my toy" boy.

A boy with green eyes, a boy who always cries, and a boy who tells the B-I-G-G-E-S-T lies!

A tough boy. A funny boy. A boy getting into trouble. A set of twin boys, "It's like seeing double!"

A boy with two moms, now that has to be cool. A boy on the slide, never playing by the rules.

A boy being silly, he gets all the attention. A boy in the principal's office with a three day suspension.

A boy getting sick on that bumpy hay ride. A boy who wets his pants that's trying to hide.

A boy answering a question when the teacher calls his name. An athletic boy winning the baseball game.

A boy who talks too much,
and one who barely speaks. A boy who knows a lot
and hangs out with the geeks.

A boy who likes to rap, and listens to rock and roll. A boy who likes heavy metal, and one who digs soul.

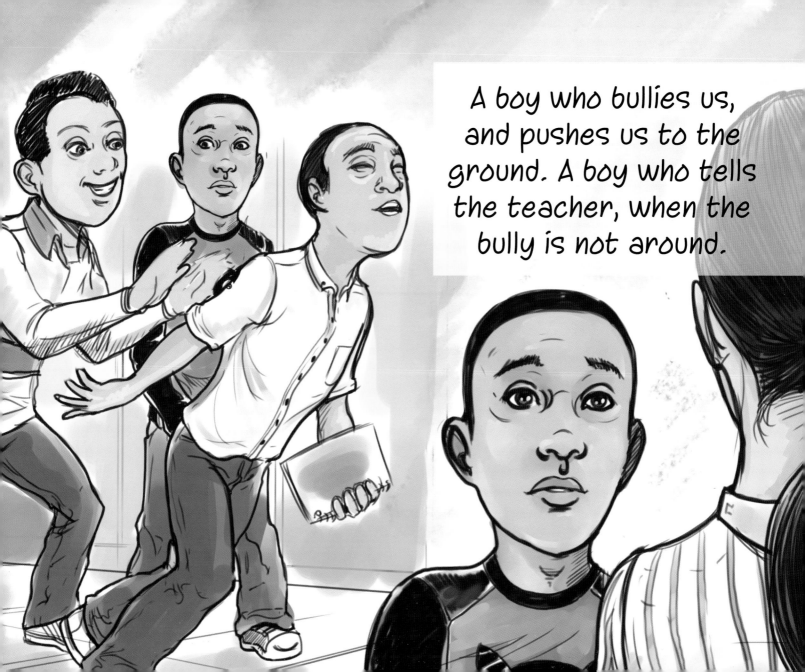

It doesn't matter how you look,
or the things you like to do. Just enjoy being a boy
your whole life through.

As you get older, and life gets really tough.
Always remind yourself of all your cool boy stuff.

QUESTIONS

Now that you have read Miguel's Amazing Book Adventure, please answer the following questions to see how much you have learned about Miguel, and his amazing friends:

1. Why wasn't Miguel allowed to go outside?

2. Describe Miguel's room. Was it clean or messy?

3. What did Miguel discover when the book fell off his bookshelf?

4. Describe some of the characters in the book.

5. What do all the characters in the book have in common?